W9-BFZ-713

10/19

*This book is dedicated to my syilx
niece and nephew, Canyon and Innasynce*

Text and illustrations copyright © 2019 Clayton Gauthier
Translation copyright © 2019 Danny Alexis and Theresa Austin

All rights reserved. No part of this publication may be reproduced or transmitted in any form or by any means, electronic or mechanical, including photocopying, recording or by any information storage and retrieval system now known or to be invented, without permission in writing from the publisher.

Cataloguing in Publication information available from Library and Archives Canada

ISBN 978-1-926886-57-2 (hardcover)

Library of Congress Control Number: 2019936377
Simultaneously published in Canada and the United States in 2019

Summary: A mother bear takes her cubs out on the land to teach them how to survive.

We acknowledge the support of the Canada Council for the Arts, which last year invested $157 million to bring the arts to Canadians throughout the country. Nous remercions le Conseil des arts du Canada de son soutien. L'an dernier, le Conseil a investi 157 millions de dollars pour mettre de l'art dans la vie des Canadiennes et des Canadiens de tout le pays. We acknowledge the support of the Province of British Columbia through the British Columbia Arts Council.

Theytus Books
theytus.com

Printed and bound in Canada.

22 21 20 19 • 4 3 2 1

SUS YOO
THE BEAR'S
MEDICINE

WRITTEN AND ILLUSTRATED BY
CLAYTON GAUTHIER

DAKELH TRANSLATION BY
DANNY ALEXIS AND
THERESA AUSTIN

THEYTUS BOOKS
schchechmala children's series

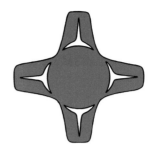

Net'a k'ut sa whunulwus
whe ts'ezninde

The light warms our backs as we wake.

'Awhulhdzin 'uts'ulh'en-i ts'uhoont'i'

We are grateful for each breath we take.

Dzulh hanasja 'et duchunyoo nuyeh

**We wander down the mountainside
to where the medicine grows.**

'Andit danghun 'uhoont'oh 'et
huwa ts'uhoont'i' too ts'utnai

**We love each drink we take,
giving thanks as the season awakes.**

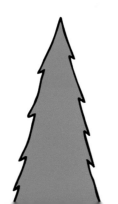

Ts'u'alh hukw'elh'az nela ts'udlat

We clean our paws as the
next meal awaits.

Tl'o ghih bulh 'u'alh 'inke'e 'unisdai

The grass and roots we share make us healthy.

Nuts'uwhulyeh 'ink'e
'utsiyanne 'oya whehudulh

**Playing in the grass, we watch
the Grandfathers pass.**

'Ahoolhdzin hoonzoo 'et
huwa ts'uhoont'i'

We walk in beauty every day,
giving thanks in every way.

Ts'iyawh lhundot'en-i nek'una 'unt'oh

**Sweet tastes of colours are
a part of our culture.**

Netso whudilhdzulh–
ne buk'oh nuts'udilh

The trail we walk on today,
our ancestors have shown us the way.

Nenateneke 'ilhunahodulh

We gather together with
our strong bloodlines.

Nyoone 'azde haindli-ne buzdilhti'

We greet new family with honour.

Nek'eke-ne cha 'uhu'alh

Our friends clean up what
is left to share.

Sa 'utsulyaz whe nulwus

The Sun shares his warmth
for a short time.

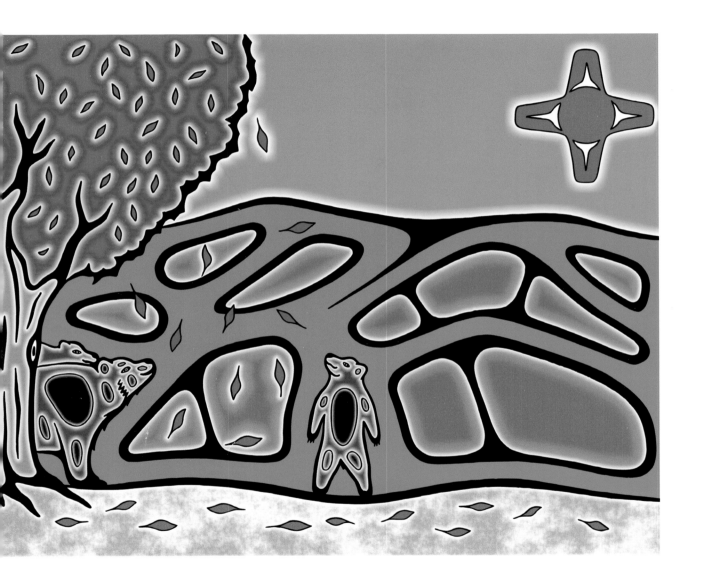

Neyoo' yus k'wijaz te
oot'ah ts'e nulwus

**The white blanket will keep
our medicine warm.**

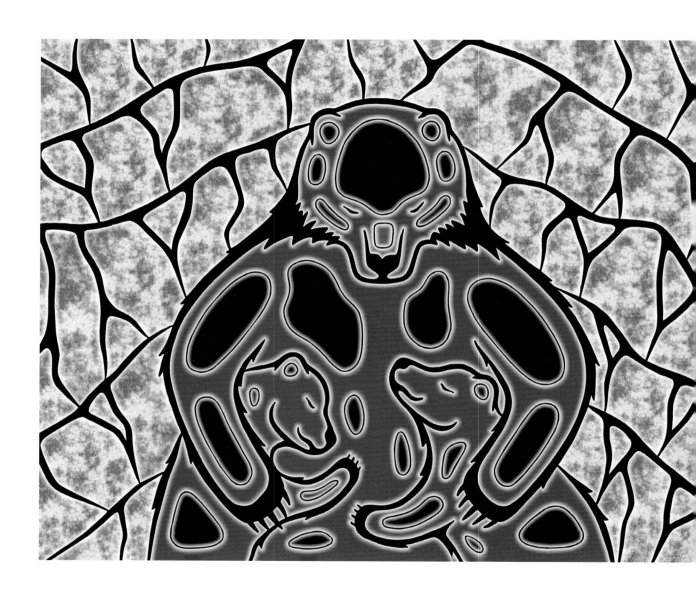

Yunk'ut yoo' ook'wets'intsi'

We love our Mothers'
medicine like no other.